Level 3 is ideal for children who are developing reading comp... stamina, and who are eager to read longer stories with a wider vocabulary.

Special features:

Detailed pictures for added interest and discussion

The witch locked Rapunzel high up in a tower. The tower had no door, just one window, for Rapunzel to look out.

Simple story structure

As he fell, the prince hurt his eyes on some thorns.

"Help!" he cried. "I cannot see." Rapunzel wanted to help the prince, but the witch took her away.

Wider vocabulary, reinforced through repetition

Longer sentences

Educational Consultant: Geraldine Taylor

A catalogue record for this book is available from the British Library

Published by Ladybird Books Ltd
80 Strand, London, WC2R 0RL
A Penguin Company

001 - 10 - 9 8 7 6 5 4 3 2 1
© LADYBIRD BOOKS LTD MMXI
Ladybird, Read It Yourself and the Ladybird Logo are registered or
unregistered trade marks of Ladybird Books Limited.

ISBN: 978-1-40930-362-6

Printed in China

This book belongs to:

CRT

....

Note to parents and carers

Read it yourself is a series of classic, traditional tales, written in a simple way to give children a confident and successful start to reading.

Each book is carefully structured to include many high-frequency words that are vital for first reading. The sentences on each page are supported closely by pictures to help with reading, and to offer lively details to talk about.

The books are graded into four levels that progressively introduce wider vocabulary and longer stories as a reader's ability grows.

Ideas for use

- Ask how your child would like to approach reading at this stage. Would he prefer to hear you read the story first, or would he like to read the story to you and see how he gets on?

- Help him to sound out any words he does not know.

- Developing readers can be concentrating so hard on the words that they sometimes don't fully grasp the meaning of what they're reading. Answering the puzzle questions on pages 46 and 47 will help with understanding.

For more information and advice, visit www.ladybird.com/readityourself

Rapunzel

Illustrated by Tamsin Hinrichsen

One day, a man and his wife were walking past a witch's garden. They were so hungry that they took some of the witch's lettuce.

Soon, they were hungry again, and the man went to the witch's garden for more lettuce. But this time, the witch saw him.

"You will be punished for taking my lettuce," said the witch. "I will take your first baby away from you."

Not long after, the man
and his wife had a baby girl.
The witch came and took
her away.

"I will call you Rapunzel,"
she said.

The witch locked Rapunzel high up in a tower. The tower had no door, just one window, for Rapunzel to look out.

Every day, the witch came to see Rapunzel.

She called up to the window, "Rapunzel, Rapunzel, let down your hair."

And Rapunzel threw her long, golden hair out of the window for the witch to climb up.

One day, a prince was walking past the tower. He heard a girl singing, and saw Rapunzel at the window.

Then the witch came.

The prince heard her call to Rapunzel, and saw her climb up Rapunzel's golden hair.

After the witch had gone
away, the prince went
to the tower and called,
"Rapunzel, Rapunzel,
let down your hair."

And Rapunzel threw her
golden hair out of the window
for the prince to climb up.

The prince and Rapunzel talked for a very long time.

The prince said, "You are too beautiful to be locked up all alone. I will help you to escape."

The next day, the witch came to see Rapunzel. As she was climbing up, the witch hurt Rapunzel.

"Ouch!" said Rapunzel. "The prince did not hurt me as he climbed up."

The witch was very angry.
To punish Rapunzel, the
witch cut off all her
beautiful hair.

The next day, the prince
went to see Rapunzel again.

He called up to the window,
"Rapunzel, Rapunzel,
let down your hair."
And he waited.

Soon, Rapunzel's beautiful golden hair came down from the window, and the prince climbed up.

To his surprise, the witch was waiting at the window. She threw the prince from the tower.

As he fell, the prince hurt his eyes on some thorns.

"Help!" he cried. "I cannot see." Rapunzel wanted to help the prince, but the witch took her away.

The prince went everywhere searching for Rapunzel, but he couldn't find her.

35

Then one day, the prince
heard a girl singing.

"Rapunzel," he cried.
"Is it you?"

"Yes," said Rapunzel.

Rapunzel was so happy to see
the prince that she started
to cry. Her tears fell into the
prince's eyes, and all at once,
he could see again.

Rapunzel said that the witch was dead. She would never be locked up in the tower ever again. She had been singing because she was so happy.

The prince took Rapunzel
away to his palace.
Very soon, they were
married, and everyone
talked happily of the
Princess Rapunzel.

So Rapunzel and her prince
lived happily ever after.

How much do you remember about the story of Rapunzel? Answer these questions and find out!

- What did the man and his wife take from the witch's garden?

- Where did the witch keep Rapunzel prisoner?

- How did the witch and the prince climb up to see Rapunzel?

- What did the prince hurt when he fell from the tower?

- How did the prince find Rapunzel again?

Look at the different story sentences and match them to the people who said them.

"You are too beautiful to be locked up all alone. I will help you to escape."

"You will be punished for taking my lettuce."

"Ouch! The prince did not hurt me as he climbed up."

Read it yourself
with Ladybird

The Three Billy Goats Gruff

Cinderella

Little Red Hen

Goldilocks and the Three Bears

The Enormous Turnip

The Magic Porridge Pot

The Ugly Duckling

The Emperor's New Clothes

The Gingerbread Man

Sleeping Beauty

Little Red Riding Hood

Town Mouse and Country Mouse

Sly Fox and Red Hen

The Three Little Pigs

Chicken Licken

Rumpelstiltskin

The Elves and the Shoemaker

Jack and the Beanstalk

Hansel and Gretel

Rapunzel

The Pied Piper of Hamelin

The Wizard of Oz

Heidi

Snow White and the Seven Dwarfs

Collect all the titles in the series.